MORALS

Also in the series

Fartin' Martin Sidebottom is a boy who can't stop breaking wind -
and joins a brass band conducted by The Devil.

Nose-picker Nick can't stop picking his nose -
and ends up inside his own nose and having a terrifying confrontation with The Bogeyman.

Grubby Joe Grub refuses to get washed -
and turns into a dirty pig. He's taken off to the abattoir, only to be saved in the nick of time.

Scary Hairy Mary is a warning to anyone who doesn't brush their hair -
poor Mary gets lost in a frightening jungle.

Excessively Messy Bessie won't keep her bedroom tidy -
and finds herself in the biggest mess of her life at Devil's Dump.

Chilly Billy Winters refuses to wrap up warm -
and is abducted by a gang of zombie snowmen.

Gobby Nobby Robinson can't stop talking -
and is caught in a deadly mouth-trap.

Smelly Simon Smedley won't change his socks -
So Bigfoot pays a visit.

Fidgety Bridget Wrigglesworth has ants in her pants and can't keep still in class -
So The Anthill Mob come calling.

ISBN - 978-1-908211-19-4

First Published in Great Britain in 2013 by Pro-actif Communications
Cameron House, 42 Swinburne Road, Darlington, Co Durham DL3 7TD
Email: books@carpetbombingculture.co.uk
Pro-actif Communications

www.monstrousmorals.co.uk

Ruth Black

This is the tooth, the whole tooth and nothing but the tooth, so help my gob

There was never a girl with teeth quite so rotten,
Or, if there was, she's long been forgotten.
No one was worse than black-toothed Ruth Black,
For using a toothbrush and battling plaque.

She was clever and loving, sweet-natured and gentle,
But a walking disaster with anything dental.
All children need pushing - but the trouble in Ruth's case,
Was a hatred of brushing and all brands of toothpaste.

The result was a mouth like a mine full of coal,
Every tooth in her head had a crack or a hole.
They quickly turned yellow, then treacly brown,
Coated in food that had not made it down.

Andrew Wilson, the dentist, just never stopped drilling,
Ruth's aching gnashers needed filling and filling.
The holes kept on growing, deeper and wider,
Til one day Mr Wilson fell head-first inside her.

Then blacker and blacker as the weeks and months passed,
Those who came close got a terrible blast,
Of bad breath so horrid I swear hand on heart,
It was worse than the stench of an elephant's fart.

Into the cavity's darkness he dived,
He might well have perished but he somehow survived.
What a narrow escape, it was such a close call,
As old mashed potato cushioned his fall.

He was down there for weeks and would have been dead,
Except for the scraps that kept him well fed.
Decomposed bits of grub were the only salvation,
Saving the dentist from certain starvation.

Left-over bacon,
pork pies, and baked beans,
Were eaten, though festering,
mouldy and green.
In the end, he was desperate,
getting madder and madder,
So he climbed out by using
a spaghetti hoop ladder.

He retired the next day having had so much grief,
And so glad to escape by the skin of his teeth.
But the nightmare was only just starting for Ruth,
The real horror began when she lost her first tooth.

It had wibbled and wobbled and hung on by a thread,
Ruth poked it and prodded until her mouth bled.
When it finally came out, all black and decayed,
She remembered the money her brother had made.

Now, George was a good boy, his teeth were all white,
So he'd get his reward 'neath his pillow at night.
Tooth fairies are beautiful, delicate things,
With silky white gowns and silvery wings.

They fly down from the stars, twinkling in space,
And take teeth away, leaving coins in their place.
They use them for castles which shimmer like pearls,
Up in the sky, in the tooth fairies' world.

But Ruth was a different kettle of fish,
She laid her tooth on her bed and made a big wish.
"A tooth for a pound" seemed quite a fair deal,
But what happened next seemed terribly real.

In the darkness, she thought she could hear something odd,
A buzz that grew louder and then OH MY GOD!
Her bedroom was swarming and Ruth was struck dumb,
Horror of horrors, the tooth devils had come.

Tooth devils are the ugliest, blood-sucking creatures,
They spread fear in young hearts with their sinister features.
They have large bat-like ears and razor-sharp fangs,
They have bulging red eyes and fly round in gangs.

With black leathery wings, pure evil in flight,
They dart around bedrooms, preparing to bite.
They can never be beaten, there's just far too many,
They steal teeth and pay nothing, not even a penny.

She fought tooth and nail but what were her chances?
With an enemy armed with tooth-picks for lances.
They stabbed at her, spat at her, pulled at her hair,
They grabbed the black tooth, but it didn't stop there.

Poor little Ruth was caught in a right mess!
As thousands of devils grabbed a piece of her nightdress.
Out through the window, they carried poor Ruth,
She'd been kidnapped by devils, that's the terrible truth.

They flew through the dark and into a wood,
Ruth wriggled like crazy but it was no good.
Deeper and deeper through the forest of pines,
Til they came to the site of an old disused mine.

They followed its shaft and the air became colder,
Castles appeared, built with incisors and molars.
The teeth were all blackened, steaming and stinking,
Surrounded by moats with poisoned black ink in.

She was taken inside the biggest castle of all,
Then locked in a dungeon with ebony walls.
A long way from home and deep underground,
Ruth's cries for help were a pitiful sound:

"Please let me out, don't leave me this way,
I promise to brush at least twice a day."
But it was too late to turn over a new leaf,
Ruth was left on her own, to rot like her teeth.

As she prepared for another night in her cage,
Ruth lost her mind and flew into a rage.
She went into a fit of shrieking and screaming,
And when she awoke, she thought she'd been dreaming.

There'd been a white flash - and there was Kathleen,
She'd swooped to the rescue, The Tooth Fairy Queen.
"Don't worry," she whispered, "I'll soon get you back,"
And that's when the guards launched a frantic attack.

A hundred tooth devils with deadly fangs bared,
Flew in for the kill but The Queen was prepared.
She broke into a smile so dazzling and bright,
The Tooth Devils were blinded and gave up the fight.

The next thing Ruth knew, she was back in her bed.
And guess the first thought that entered her head?
She ran to the bathroom in a desperate rush,
To give every last tooth a floss and a brush.

From that day to this, she's never had to be told,
For brushing her teeth, our Ruth's good as gold.
Morning or night-time, she's ever so willing,
There's been no more tooth-ache, not even a filling.

Her teeth are pure white,
the best by a mile,
The world is lit up
by her magical smile.
As for her nightmares,
they've come to an end,
No more devils, just fairies,
with money to spend.